.

Thank you
for your encouragement

Another Tapestry Of Words

Rona V Flynn

Index

A Verse or Two

A verse or two, a word, a song
puts away a tiring day
and lifts our mood to float along
mind's rivers where we sail away.

Rona V Flynn

Queen Elizabeth II
Elizabeth Alexandra Mary Windsor
21st April 1926 ~ 8th September 2022

Thank you Ma-am for Everything

I knew a Queen who knew James Bond,
she kept marmalade butties in her bag.
Her eyes twinkled, her laugh tinkled
and she roared at the funniest gags.

I knew a Queen who worked her long life
and her smile lit up the room.
She gave her years through laughs and tears
bringing light into the gloom.

I knew a Queen who loved the hills
and moors of the Scottish highs.
She was neat and small but ten feet tall,
and sweet and kind and wise.

I knew a Queen who listened well
when chatting face to face,
when she fixed their eyes, she hypnotized.
She had get up and go and pace.

When she finally came to her journey's end
the nation paused to weep.
Our hearts were sore, we could ask no more
of a Queen who deserved to sleep.

Rona V Flynn

Sweet Contradiction

Unavoidable sweet contradiction,
the light and dark of spring
kissing our cheeks with golden warmth
reminiscent of high summer.
Inescapable cool unpredicted
darkened light of the season,
when shadows bite with wintry winds
resisting sunlight's shimmer.

Rona V Flynn

Happy Circumstance

Be that special someone
in someone else's day.
Make a sweet surprise that brings
a smile along their way.
Be their happy circumstance
just at the right time,
a little sprinkled magic
without reason, and no rhyme.

A scrap of thoughtful sharing
takes a moment, maybe two
but may touch a soul in some way
that is far too overdue.
Your heart will smile and quicken
when you secretly create
a sweet memory for someone
randomly, and captivate.

Rona V Flynn

The House that Smiles

I live in a house that smiles.
It's small and neat and warm and sweet.
I've lived here for a while.

My comfy sofa swoons
with worn-out springs that often sing
a little bit out of tune.

I have a little garden too.
What I've got is a squarish plot
with flowers ~ quite a few.

Rona V Flynn

In the background of this picture stands
Ainscough Mill, West Lancs, UK.
Built in 1815 beside the canal,
this mill is now filled with people
living in comfortable apartments
surrounded by
nature and fresh skies.

The Mill

When scraps of downy cotton chase the breeze
round cold tall chimneys
they glimpse tidy walls filled with warmth
and cosy comfort.
Silver windows open wide
to clear blue skies breathing easy
over nature in its glory.
Today is a new day.

Rona V Flynn

An abundance of spiky thorns and soft petals,
a rose with a beautiful fragrance

Tender Hearts

When our hearts are broken
they expose a deep well
where pain and sorrow mingle.
Drawn by undercurrents
we hold on awash,
growing stronger and wiser
as new threads weave
healing and understanding…
completing us
a little more
every time
every time
every time
every time
every time
every time
every time
every…
…

Rona V Flynn

Sensing the Earth

Lively fingers toing and froing,
Pulling, pushing,
sweeping and hoeing.

Enjoying the birdsong, breathing fresh air.
Cutting off branches
to mend wear and tear.

Minding the insects, bees and the like.
Watching the greenfinch,
robin and shrike.

Planting, uprooting, sensing the earth.
Trees turning gold
before sleep and rebirth.

Concentration honed for the task.
Steely dark sky.
Hot tea from the flask.

Skirting perfection leaves room for all kinds.
Preparing for winter
as Autumn unwinds.

Rona V Flynn

Riverman

He saw the Riverman that day
and talked about the river's time.
He mused on words he'd yet to write
and dreamed of freedom down the line.

His velvet voice, though fragile soft,
carried far his haunting tune
of life and love and harvest time,
of lilac spring and rose pink moon.

The Riverman knew everything
about the way the river winds
and listened to the thoughts and plans
meandering within his mind.

They met again when dusk befell,
where clear as glass cool waters run,
then quietly fading into night
his game was lost, the day was done.

Rona V Flynn

Nick Drake
1948 – 1974

Stained Glass Jester
created by Clare.

Dancing Jester

When the sun comes out
the Jester passes by,
dancing on the sideboard
with a twinkle in his eye.
His brightly painted coat
brings a smile and merry cheer
and his twists and his turns
make a happy atmosphere.

As the long hours pass
so he will pass by too,
showing off his colours
and his hat of every hue.
With a nod and a wink
as twilight gently falls
he fades into the darkness
til tomorrow's sunrise calls.

Rona V Flynn

For Clare

High on a Hill

Battered by winds high on a hill
I stand my ground and you blow harder still.
Breath taken away by unstoppable course
of incredible power. Wild fearsome force
blow through me, within me, bleak and raw.
Ravish the day, make way for more.
Wake me and move me, stir me, revive.
What a beautiful view. Never felt so alive.

Rona V Flynn

I Do Wish

I do wish I had ears to hear
the frost form on the pane.
Sun may briefly warm it
but the chill reweaves again.
Crisp and sharpened icy cold
crystals are reborn
to flow and spin their beauty
in the frost of winter's dawn.

Rona V Flynn

Shenanigans

Away with your shenanigans.
What a delightful word.
Silliness and high jinks,
chaotic and absurd.
Naughtiness and clowning,
getting into trouble.
Trifles, tricks and follies.
Shambles, mess and muddle.

Rona V Flynn

Eve

Running through grasses
she searches and follows
through forests and woodland,
moorland and hills.
Plunging off clifftops
to swim through the valleys,
exploring the grasslands,
replenishing spills.

Sunlight sparkles
off ripples and splashes.
Sprinkles of moonlight
dance through the night.
Streaming through meadows
she runs through the reedbeds,
clear as crystal catching the light.

Greeting the morning,
she meets every sunrise
sparking new life
as she goes on her way.
Pausing and musing
through midnight meanders,
the circle completing
through day, night and day.

Rona V Flynn

Life's too Short,
don't underestimate.
If there's something on your mind,
may come a time when it's too late.

Rona V Flynn

Rose and Gio

Her dancing was perfection.
Music filled our captive ear.
Like breath of silk, she floated
effortlessly sheer,
giving so completely
of a spirit free and rare.
When the room fell silent
starlit magic filled the air.
The spell was overwhelming,
our hearts were touched profound.
In awe we watched and listened
to the message without sound.

Rona V Flynn

Rose and Giovanni
Strictly Come Dancing, May, 2022

This Old Thing?

What, this old thing?
It was in the drawer,
I'd forgotten all about it.
It's something I once wore.
Threadbare and dated
it's been and it's gone.
It's lost all its glory,
had its day in the sun.

But *this*. Now this is something
I slipped into when I woke.
Don't you just love it,
it's so different. It's bespoke.
It changes with the light
and I've had it a long time.
I've never seen another
anywhere. It's just divine.

It's timeless in its detail
as you'll see if you draw near.
Delicate yet lasting
and a treasure I hold dear.
This, I'll keep forever ~
well as long as if I can.
Come closer, feel the softness,
it's a one-off ~ Artisan.

Fine wine once consumed
is never ever seen again.
Old masters lie in darkened rooms,
hidden way back when.
But this, a thing of beauty
you can touch and hold and see.
This will *never* lose its glory
and it wears just perfectly.

Rona V Flynn

Hitching a Ride

It was a smooth ride
with some exec drivin' in style.
It was silent inside
and glided swiftly mile after mile.
It was off the page,
room in the back for two, three more.
Seats were leather beige
and fancy wood lay in the doors.
He had a quiet touch
but he smiled sometimes and listened.
We said thank you very much.
He streaked away, the silver glistened.

Rona V Flynn

Tír na nÓg.

There is a place they say
where age has never been
and life is filled with joy,
delight and bliss.
It may be far
or near enough to touch,
the hidden paradise
beyond the mist.

Tír na nÓg.
A place of magic and of wonder
is where they dwell
in everlight.
None can see
unless granted leave to be
in the enchanted world of
timeless nevernight.

Rona V Flynn

The Celtic myth of Tír na nÓg tells us of
a mysterious Otherworld of beauty and
abundance.
A place where time passes not,
and inhabitants never age.

35

Where Did They Go

Did someone take the plush velvet
and shake it outrageously fierce.
Gone are the multitudes lighting the sky
midst the darkness round heavenly spheres.
Once was a time of inky black
with stars shining clear and bright.
It is for the night to be flooded with dark
and day to be flooded with light.

Rona V Flynn

Myfanwy Fychan of Castell Dinas Brân

Myfanwy, my Myfanwy.
How he loved her face so fair
and the blush of her soft cheeks
encircled by her raven hair.

Hywel, a Welsh poet
who had watched her from afar
was besotted by her beauty
shining bright as any star.

He wooed and thought he'd won her
until that wretched day
when she favoured but another
and her face was turned away.

He pined all day and night.
Bereft, he longed to see her care.
He yearned for his belovèd's
gaze and shock of midnight hair.

Each day without Myfanwy
was too cruel to suffer long
but his love it never faded
and he never lost her song.

Some say they still can hear him
there amid the Castle trees
where echoes of her name
will gently sing upon the breeze.

His heart will ever mourn her,
his soul forever call.
Though the Castle lies in ruins
his love will transcend all.

Rona V Flynn

The legend of penniless Welsh bard
Hywel ap Einion Llygliw.
He was a humble man who fell
in love with the daughter of an Earl.
Myfanwy was a vain woman,
refusing any man
unable to truly express her beauty
through music and verse.
Hywel was
given permission to sing his songs to her
and she listened as he sang and played the harp.
He thought he had won her heart but
along came a rich, eloquent gentleman
who stole her gaze away
and he was left broken-hearted.
The Welsh-built castle dates back to the 13th Century
and is believed to have been built
on the site of an Iron Age hillfort.
The ruins still lie in North Wales
in the town of Llangollen.

Cake for Breakfast

A sunny seat by the window.
Glinting cars dip into shade.
Shoppers stroll in morning sun.
Twitching noses poke through the door.
Simon and Garfunkel ease in the day.
Tangy lemon cake, yellow and sweet.
Coffee ignites sleepy senses.
Teaspoons tinkle in the background
as I begin to seize the day.

Rona V Flynn

Greedy Bear and the Sunflowers

Given to having his way
the big bear peered through the trees.
He had been watching for a while,
what he saw did not appease.

Happy sunflowers filled the fields
and they were everywhere,
dancing and singing in sunshine
without fear or care.

He stamped his foot and stamped again.
He *wanted* them right *now*
and stewing in his own dark thoughts
he'd make them his somehow.

Breaking through the borders
after watching them for long
He ran amok through everything,
no thought for right nor wrong.

The lofty sunflowers once so tall
lay crushed and trodden, there
in the dirt all broken
because of Greedy Bear.

He roared when he thought he'd finished
but the flowers rose once more.
The harder he stamped, the faster they grew.
It chilled him to the core.

No matter what, sunflowers would rise
mid chaos all around.
Together they stood tall and strong
and they took back their ground.

The bear resented their resolve
for they would not give in.
Nothing seemed to stop them.
They were not an easy win.

At last the bear was on the run,
ousted, finished, beat.
He stamped his foot, he was undone,
chastened by defeat.

Rona V Flynn

Magpies

Mr & Mrs Magpie
crossed the road on foot.
He said *See, just follow me!*
but Mrs? she stayed put.

He strode across the empty road
and almost reached half-way.
The green light shone, his chance was gone,
back he ran without delay.

Next red lights I watched to see,
truly mystified.
They strolled as a pair with confident air
and crossed to the other side.

They *walked* across a busy road!
I beg the question, *Why!*
Of all odd things, they had their wings,
why did they not just *fly!*

Rona V Flynn

True story!

Deep and Wide

Take me to the desert
where sun beats on the lime
and white rocks pierce my eyes with shards
of brilliant opaline.

Fly me to the high place
where air is arid dry
and stillness holds the scorching heat
raining from the sky.

Walk me to the soft sea
of silk and satin plush
to lay upon the waters
in the silence of the hush.

Sail me to the oceans
of deep and high and wide.
Bring me to that heavy place
and I'll be satisfied.

Rona V Flynn

The Art Boat

Hippy Boats

What a beautiful day, the sun is high
and the hippy boats are passing by
with purple gems, old candlesticks,
a curious eclectic mix
of sunshine dresses and baggy pants,
caught up by the breeze they swing and dance.
The Art Boat with its painted scenes
of bridges, boats and snowy fields,
old stone walls, canal side pubs,
fishermen sitting with coffee mugs.
When comes the time to stow away
their wares at close of a busy day,
magically they fit inside
the tiny home where they reside.
Belongings stark, of strappings freed
where all they have is all they need,
they live and work and breathe afloat
both night and day on their narrowboat.

Rona V Flynn

Kiss the Moon

Twilight murmurs softly
drawing down the end of day,
whispering sweet nothings
as the night goes on its way.
Cool air gently drifts
beneath the tiny specks of light
until the morning when the sunshine
comes to kiss the moon goodnight.

Rona V Flynn

We feel the pain and joy of those closest
to our hearts
as if it were our own.

If you Break

If you break, I am broken.
If you cry, I will weep.
If you are blue, I feel sad.

If you ache, I am sore.
If you suffer, I will wane.
If you fear, I feel powerless.

If you smile, I am glad.
If you flourish, I will thrive.
If you are happy, I feel joy.

Rona V Flynn

Just a moment

It's difficult to speculate
how little we all know.
A moment lasts a lifetime,
a lifetime but a mo.
For they are life's non-quantifiable
smidgeons of time.
The sum of moments in a day
is tricky to define.

A wise man* many years ago
said he'd worked it out.
He fixed his Bede-y eye and
he said this ~
> *I have no doubt*
> *there's forty in an hour or so,*
> *but don't be too precise.*
> *Give or take if night or day ~*
and that was his advice.

*St Bede

Precious moments fill our hearts,
imparting sweet delight.
Forever they will keep us warm
through darkest winters nights.
A moment, down cannot be tied,
they're fanciful and free,
for measuring a moment's
an impossibility.

Rona V Flynn

Hot Chocolate and Sandwiches

This poem is a story in itself but also continues the tale 'If Only' from Poetry Two.

She sat down on the bench
to feed the geese and ducks some bread
and pulled her hat over her ears.
Her nose was getting red.

Come rain or shine she sat there
with her backpack and a flask,
The bench beside the duck pond
was her favourite Monday task.

Cheese and pickle sandwiches
with oat milk chocolate, hot,
followed by a flapjack.
Just the job to hit the spot.

This week she had noticed
an old familiar form
seated just across the way.
It made her heart feel warm.

He looks just the same, she thought.
I loved his messy hair.
Then she threw more bread and chuckled,
he was never debonair.

I can't believe we never passed
each other in the street.
I wonder if he's married.
Cold was getting to her feet.

Three years had passed since she'd last seen
the man sat over there.
She sometimes thought about him
and the things she didn't dare.

~

The man across the way thought
'Must be ages since we sat
in the Happy Place Cafe
then she was gone and that was that!

That night his sister rang him
and he talked about his day.
She gave some wise words of advice.
He knew that's what she'd say.

Each day he went back to the park
but never saw her there.
He thought about the caff
and how he loved her auburn hair.

Monday came and off she set.
The sun feels warm today.
A skip was springing light her step,
she smiled along the way.

No sandwiches were in her bag,
no flask to keep her warm.
Today she would lunch somewhere else.
It's good to change my norm.

The waitress there was just the same
except her hair was blue.
'Hello' she laughed. 'Were have you been!'
It's good to see you too.

Hot chocolate please with oat milk,
soup and chunky bread...
and can I have a flapjack.
'Coming up!' she said.

It seemed so very long ago.
She thought about that day
and the fancy blonde, the whirlwind
who had swept her dreams away.

She sighed and thought
This is so nice, it feels like coming home.
The waitress brought her order
and a treat of honeycomb.

The music was so soothing
as she sipped her chocolate mug.
Her hat and scarf were laid aside,
the caff was warm and snug.

She slowly started drifting
in and out of cosy doze,
til someone broke her daydream.
You've got chocolate on your nose.

Embarrassed, she said *Sorry!*
Gosh, I almost nodded… Oh!
He said *Erm, may I join you?*
She said *Yes of course…* aglow.

He ordered soup and chunky bread,
coffee and éclair.
They never stopped their talking,
who'd have thought they'd even dare.

The waitress leaned upon her bench
all misty-eyed and smiles.
*They're just **made** to be together,*
I could tell for miles and miles.

Rona V Flynn

The Beautiful Dream

Something took hold of my heart
and squeezed it a little with love.
That warm tender touch moved me so much
as tears bathed in wistfulness of…

That time is now way in the past.
Long gone is the beautiful dream
of living in peace, all fighting to cease
when *make love not war* reigned supreme.

With softening hearts and new hope
a passion swept through the earth.
Folk were free-giving, creating and living
a movement of change and rebirth.

Songs filled with promise anew
spread through the throngs liberally.
Love undisciplined spread like a fresh wind
precious moments in our history.

Rona V Flynn

Ebb and Flow

Ebbs and flows
and tos' and froes.
Yeas and noes
and in the throes.
It happens like that
with ebbs and flows.

Highs and lows
and reaps and sows.
Friends and foes,
open and close.
Life just goes
and the flow just flows.

Who'd suppose
such joys and woes
and curves and blows
and fasts and slows
would sprinkle through time
such sweet rainbows.

Rona V Flynn

The Letter

He wrote a letter in his mind
to share his treasured thoughts,
crossing out and changing lines.
His words came but to naught.

He wrote a letter in his heart
with hopes he could say more,
baring all from end to start
until his soul was sore.

He penned a post card *Just a note*
to say hope you are well
but from his heart he never wrote
and doubted he should tell.

He wrote and rewrote prose anew
one thousand times and more
and yet although each jot was true
they never crossed the door.

As weeks and months and years were spent
his heart felt sore regret
for all the words he'd never sent
and words not written yet.

Rona V Flynn

Sup with Me

Come sup with me,
sit and be
in dappled shade of evening sun.
Let birdsong wash through your soul
and trickling waters soothe.

Break bread with me,
laugh and smile,
indulge in the sweet
taste of idling
where voices mingle softened by warmth.

Stay with me
to lounge and loll.
Sigh and snooze
as you rest your mind
in fading light of summer.

Rona V Flynn

Streaming

Streaming lights zip here and there
piercing cold dark winter air.
Rainbows chase along the streets
like coloured lights in autumn's fair.

Wispy sprinkles of soft snow
meet the wet dark roads below.
We sail beneath a troubled sky
as bright lights guide us through the flow.

Rona V Flynn

The Last Goodbye

His voice resounded through their bones,
their spirit drawn by mournful tones.
With every tear, their sore hearts bled
for every word left still unsaid.

Rona V Flynn

Hurry Little One

Hurry little one,
soar like a whisper
floating on soft down.
Swoop soundless,
eyes wide open
skim the dusky ground.
Take supper home
to fill hungry mouths
then sleep til morning sounds.

Rona V Flynn

Wheel Within a Wheel

Dry wood axed from seasons chills
reveals the soft green shoots.
A little here and there will see
off winter's absolute.
A small drop in the ocean,
a wheel within a wheel.
The cold winds now are changing
and the sap begins to heal.

Rona V Flynn

Time Flies

Time flies unbelievably so.
Who thought it would come and go
so quick. In the merest blink of an eye
memories form, then pass us by.

Time flies in old photographs,
black and white as we lived our laughs.
Recollections accumulate
of life long spent. Time doesn't wait.

Time flies as we reminisce
on friends and school and first love's kiss.
Let's rock when birthdays come to call,
take hold of life, embrace it all.

Rona V Flynn

Summer's Sleeping

Heavens slowly fade and harden,
cooler fingers stretch the sky.
Golden breath ignites the blazing
trees before their last goodbye.
Season's time has come for turning.
Melancholy fills the air.
Starkened shadows scape the skyline
painting colours sparse and bare.
Swift the trees succumb to darkness,
standing bleak within the gloom.
Summer's sleeping, breathing softly.
Autumn will be leaving soon.

Rona V Flynn

Tie it Off

If it's finished, let it be.
Close the door, cut it free.
If it's done, wipe it out.
No ifs or buts or whys or doubts.

Rona V Flynn

Grey Days

If it's a dull and cloudy day
go for a walk, blow the blues away.
Feed the ducks and have a chat.
Whisper to a wayward cat.
Stop to sniff a blossom tree.
Marvel at a bumblebee.
Look for ripples made by fish.
Count the magpies, make a wish.
Sit on a bench and watch the world,
note the way a cloud unfurls.
Wave the wild geese on their away.
Enjoy your dull and cloudy day.

Rona V Flynn

Wild Stallions

Rearing stallions catch
the sun in drops of pearly gold.
Seizing the tide
they rise from the deep,
railing like thunder in clearest of blue.
Unstoppable they ride
with rolling foam
through breakers crashing to the shore.
They leap and fly
long manes askew,
with every wave
they gallop endless til they lie

a g a i n
o r
s
m
o o
t g o l
h d
s e n
o d d

Rona V Flynn

Adisa and Enitan

"Adisa…Adisaaaa…"

"*Stop* whispering into my *ear* Enitan, I'm trying to **sleep!**

Enitan giggled. He knew just how much it would annoy him but he delighted in whispering into his brother's ear while he was sleeping - he was much more fun when he was awake.

Scratching at the dry earth with his stick, Enitan kept an eye on their scrawny cows, singing songs he'd listened to all his life. The responsibility of watering them each morning lay with him and his older brother, who had now disappeared in search of peace and quiet.

There was good reason for Adisa to feel tired as family celebrations had continued late into the night. These were joyful occasions, when everyone came together to share and remember the old times. The evening would begin with their Grandmother performing the family ritual from her 'throne'. She would sing out in a clear voice the names of their ancestors through several generations without even having to stop and think. The name Enitan means 'Person with a long story' and Enitan knew well his story. He would listen to every name, waiting to sing and dance when his Grandmother finally called out *Enitan* at the end of a very long list. After the names, came old family tales and tribal songs reaching back hundreds of years. Although Enitan had taken himself to bed when he could no longer keep his eyes open, Adisa had barely slept.

~~~

The sun would soon be high and Enitan knew that by now they should be making their way home. Where *is* he! Stamping his feet, he let out an exaggerated growl of frustration, hoping Adisa would hear him – *wherever* he was.

After taking a deep breath he shouted one last time. *"Wake up Adisa! We need to go home!"* It was with heavy heart that he began the walk alone, keeping his cows in order along the way.

As he drew nearer to the village, he noticed it looked deserted. He felt instinctively something wasn't right. Breaking into a run he was confronted by a scene of chaos. Spilled cooking pots and a myriad of possessions lay strewn across the ground with loose beads from his mother's necklace scattered around the entrance to their home. He gasped, pausing for a moment as he tried to bring his thoughts together.

Calling out, he tripped over his mother's upturned stool as he ran inside. She was nowhere to be seen. Gently, he picked up the broken necklace, half full with the remaining beads, and turned to retrieve the others by the door. After pushing them into his pouch he stood still and listened. The silence was deafening, all he could hear was his heart pounding. Trying hard not to cry, he quickly wiped away his tears as he looked around. Leaping over the cooking pot, he bound towards tracks leading away from the village.

As swiftly as the hand covered his mouth so too did his feet fly into the air! Whoever had taken hold of him ran like the wind for what seemed like an eternity.

Finally, they fell to the ground under cover of bushes.

"Adisa!" With wide eyes and wet cheeks, he held on tight to his big brother, sobbing into his chest while he gasped to catch his breath.

Adisa put his fingers over Enitan's lips with a sharp *"Sh!"* and did so every time he tried to speak. There they lay quietly for a long time until Adisa threw himself over his little brother, whispering urgently into his ear. *"Sh, keep still!"*

~~~

Fifteen years is a long time but Adisa still scanned every new face, hoping to see Enitan's eyes looking back at him. He longed to tell him as much as he could remember about who they were and from time to time he tried to recall their Grandmother's songs and stories, sad that he had already forgotten so many names.

When he first arrived at the plantation, he was given the name Thomas…and *Thomas* he had been called ever since… Sometimes, when he lay in his bed, he ached to hear his little brother whisper *Adisa* into his ear once again. As he pondered on what might have happened to him and where he may have been taken the pain was almost too much to bear.

~~~

Somewhere far away Enitan toiled for a task master who had the right to treat him as cruelly as he saw fit. His chore of watering cows in lazy sunshine soon became a distant memory and life was hard. For a long time, he had lain awake at night quietly reciting the family names as he waited for his big brother to rescue him.

It seemed so long ago now and he often wondered where Adisa might be, pushing out of his mind the thought that he may no longer be alive. Sometimes he would imagine meeting him again and quietly whisper his name just like he used to. The years had toughened him but his heart still yearned for his family.

The day Adisa and Enitan were taken was the day life as they knew it ceased to be. In the twinkling of an eye all things familiar had gone. The earth they walked upon, the scents that surrounded them, sounds that lulled them to sleep at night and woke them in the mornings. In an instant, everything had *stopped*.

Now they awoke to a new call each morning with orders bellowed in a foreign language they had no choice but to learn.

In time, childhood memories would fade and names would be forgotten. Recollections of village life and the rich culture they knew from the day they were born would slowly slip away and their family story would eventually be lost forever…

The Embrace

Centring and standing strong
we commence our sacred song
with softened earth and moistened breath,
fusing as we coalesce.
Turning slow in warm embrace
we dance together face to face
in the flow moving as one,
singing til the labour's done.

Rona V Flynn

Valentine

What's that you say,
it's Valentine's Day
for those whose love is true.
Red roses and things
that make a heart sing
and all that hullabaloo.

Love's sweet dreams,
stars and moonbeams.
Secret cards and notes.
Sweets and chocs,
flowers in a box,
lacy petticoats.

Did you know
that true love so
needs first to come from you
… to you.

Rona V Flynn

Unravelling

I think we are unravelling
slow but sure as day,
losing stitches silent
as they slip and fall away.
Like a woolly jumper
where one hole leads to more
we're slowly disappearing
as the ocean takes the shore.

I think we are unravelling,
the earth seems really sad.
War ravages her landscapes
and the air sometimes is bad.
We need to find us some way
to knit the stitches back
with peace and conversation
to get us back on track.

We can stop unravelling
at home in our own space
by picking up the stitches,
making love more commonplace.
Intentionally trying
to hold close those who are dear,
mending where we can and
being mindful of those near.

Rona V Flynn

Sparrowhawk

Look at her,
swift and triumphant.
Posing in splendour on defeated prey
she holds tight her impressive prize.
Golden eyes dart and flash,
piercing air with keen precision.
Striped breast beats proud
as feathered confetti scatters.
Dining done she takes flight
soaring high on the warm breeze,
shadowed against evening sun.

Rona V Flynn

Summer Bride

Up-river she ambles
riding the breeze,
humming and singing
under the trees.
Sharing her beauty
she perfumes the air
with enchantment and calm,
with healing and prayer.
Her company pleases
like love woke at dawn
with sunlight's soft filter
when bringing new morn.

Rona V Flynn

CHRISTMAS BLESSINGS

May your Christmas be joyful
and filled with good cheer

May love peace and hope
bring a healthy new year

Rona & Flynn

Christmas Memories

Make some memories this Christmas.
Take a pic, capture the vibe.
Make the most of those around you
and enjoy this year's yuletide.

Rona V Flynn

Betwixt and Between

Lost in the mist we wander
from one sleep to the next
in a state of limbo
when all we do is rest.
Wishing cheer and joy
between leftovers and cake.
Lazing on the sofa
more sleeping than awake.
Cold turkey, stuffing, eggnog
for breakfast, lunch and tea.
It seems we're lost in limbo
for an eternity.
In a land of nowhere.
What day is it ~ What time.
More chocolate if you want it.
Would you like some wine?
We stir when New Year's Eve arrives.
We stop to watch the clock
as the long day finally meets its end
and we revel in the last tick tock.

Happy New Year!!

Rona V Flynn

$\longrightarrow$

I hope you enjoyed my poems and prose.

Here I am again with my fifth book of poetry.

When I sat down to write a short story in 2012, I had no idea I would end up publishing two novels and five poetry books! Life is full of surprises…

Such a lot has happened in the world over the last year and maybe in your life too – but still the world keeps turning.

Writing has been an adventure and a challenge in so many ways and I'm still really enjoying it. Here's to beginning Poetry Six sometime soon. (I never know when the first poem will be written until it just drops into my heart.)

Look after yourself ~ and thank you for reading my poems.

See you next year all being well.

Rona x

Ps. If you enjoyed this book, Poetry books 1, 2, 3 and 4 are also available.

Please turn the page for more information about poetry books and novels.

$\rightarrow$

Snippets of Reviews
for this and previous publications

Poetry Books

Bleed into the Walls
Great poem, great title.
I never thought of it like that.

Sacking and Silk
I've been there!

Wild Wood
"I love the peace and tranquillity of this poem.

What a lovely cocktail of words. The magic this Poet weaves
is so inspired and heart-warming.

Wild Stallions
This is my favourite, so atmospheric. I can
picture everything perfectly.

Daydream
This poem is so true.

Sup with Me
Just reading this poem made me relax.

Low light in September
This poem is so evocative of crisp, cold autumn.

$\rightarrow$

Damsels and Dragons
"What a beautiful poem. So full of wonderful imagery. The process is pretty amazing and the author has captured the magic and mystery very descriptively." Nature Lover.
The British Dragonfly Society liked this poem so much that they shared it on their Facebook Page.

Blackbird
"The poem entitled 'Blackbird' is beautiful and I love the author's description of its song. It is such a magical sound and she expresses it so perfectly. I also like the blackbird's eye being 'starlight cloaked in ebony velvet.' Gorgeous!"
Lesley Rawlinson, Author.

Earth's Bones

"The author shows great insight into the Earth's amazing processes in the poem 'Earth's Bones'. I love it!"
Jennifer Jones, Earth Scientist and Author.

"Some very emotive poems sparking memories; contemplation; some smiles and some sadness."
"Beautiful and sometimes poignant."
"I really like this author's poems.
This poet has a subtle use of language."
"Some poems have a spiritual feel."
"Insightful, I swear the Author is reading my mind!"

Cont'd…

Silver Key

"You will not be disappointed with this next book of The Light Keepers series! I absolutely loved it and was moved to tears in some parts and laughing out loud in others."

"Star's journey took us through magical portals, and introduced an array of new and interesting characters, including a couple on the dark side.

"I can't wait for the next book now, I loved reading about the struggle between darkness and light and the inner struggles of the characters. It's so true to life!"

"An enjoyable story, with a hint of a new adventure to come."

"They are absolutely brilliant books! I couldn't put them down as I was so excited to find out what happens next. I can't wait until my daughter is old enough to read them, I know she's going to love them."

$\rightarrow$

Star's Awakening

"The author has created a really vivid world. The book is easy to read and nicely paced."

"I thoroughly enjoyed it. It was one of those books I just wanted to keep on turning the pages to find out what was happening next."

"I thoroughly enjoyed this book. The characters were easy to visualise."

"A good story line and great characterisation."

"I was totally drawn into the life of the central family."

"It was amazing. I absolutely loved the story line and the characters!! Can't wait for the next book in the series."

"An interesting and enjoyable read, I was drawn into the story right from the beginning."

"I was intrigued, it was complex, I couldn't put it down."

Cont'd…

My novels are available on Kindle and in paperback

Two stories with just a touch of fantasy. These tales follow Star and her family through the twists and turns of family life as she becomes an adult. Old secrets are uncovered and new friends and enemies are made as their journey unfolds.

Star's Awakening and The Silver Key feature the age-old struggle between good and evil, and the family's journey through it. The tales begin in Gawswood, a close-knit community with Star's family is at the heart of it.

Star's Awakening – Lightkeepers Book One
Star's widowed father is the settle Elder. All is well, but as Star prepares for her coming of age, everything begins to change. Old enemies, the discovery of family secrets, and life-changing events lead us through their journey.

The Silver Key – Lightkeepers Book Two
The continuation of *Star's Awakening* picks up the family's tale five years later. Life in Gawswood has been good - but all is not as it seems. We watch the human condition weaving its way through the trials and tribulations that beset them. Interesting new characters join them as they search for answers and closure.

Thank you
x

Printed in Great Britain
by Amazon

24703852R00067